The Adventures of Lucy

"Good Morning Lucy"

Written By Gina Lucero
Illustrated by Gene Lucero

AuthorHouse™
1663 Liberty Drive
Bloomington, IN 47403
www.authorhouse.com
Phone: 833-262-8899

Because of the dynamic nature of the Internet, any web addresses or links contained in this book may have changed since publication and may no longer be valid. The views expressed in this work are solely those of the author and do not necessarily reflect the views of the publisher, and the publisher hereby disclaims any responsibility for them.

Any people depicted in stock imagery provided by Getty Images are models, and such images are being used for illustrative purposes only.
Certain stock imagery © Getty Images.

This book is printed on acid-free paper.

ISBN: 978-1-6655-5161-8 (sc)
ISBN: 978-1-6655-5162-5 (e)

Print information available on the last page.

Published by AuthorHouse 02/10/2022

authorHOUSE®

The Adventures of Lucy

"Good Morning Lucy"

Lucy the Beagle was an adventurous dog. She loved her walks around the community. Every morning she would hear Thomas the Rooster, and that was her cue to get up and make her rounds.

Lucy loved going and visiting all of her neighbors.

"Good morning Lucy!"
"Do you want some left over bacon and eggs?" The neighbor,Gloria would ask?

Lucy's tail would wag in excitement! She would lick the plate clean and off she would go to see the next neighbor. Before leaving,She would lick Gloria's face to say thank you and off she would go. Gloria would yell after her, "See you tomorrow, Lucy!"

"Hello Lucy!" Greeted the neighbor, Aurora! "I have some leftover pancakes for you!"

Lucy's tail would wag with excitement and she licked the plate clean. She would lick Aurora's face to say thank you. Off she would go to see the next neighbor.

Well, hello Lucy, the neighbor Josh would say! " I bet you are hungry, let me see what I have in the fridge for you." Josh came back with a fresh bone from the steak he had for dinner last night. "How about this?" he asked

Lucy's tail wagged with excitement, she gently took the bone and off she went to find a nice spot near the lake to chew on her bone.

Lucy began to chew on her bone when Ella walked by. "Well, hello Lucy!" Whatcha got there?" she asked. Lucy nudged the bone towards her.

Oh my, that looks like it will keep you busy for a few hours! "Have fun, Lucy" and Ella went about her walk, but she reached in her pocket and remembered she had placed a few dog treats in her pocket, just in case she ran into Lucy. " I almost forgot, here are a few treats for you! Enjoy!"

Lucy was sitting underneath a tall catalpa tree, enjoying the shade and she started to get sleepy. Her tummy was full, the grass was so inviting and the shade from the tree was a perfect combination for a nap. She could feel her eyes getting heavy and she shook it off, got up and started her walk.

She ran into Ranger Alex, "Hey there, Lucy!" he exclaimed "I was going to find you! I brought my lunch today and packed a little extra for you! Hop on up here and eat with me."

Lucy hopped up on the truck bed and Ranger Alex, broke off a piece of his hamburger and gave it to her.
"You sure are a great dog, you know that? "As he patted her on the head.

She finished her piece of hamburger and licked his face to thank him, and she jumped down and started to make her way back home.

By this time, her belly was so full, all she wanted to do was go home and sleep in her bed.

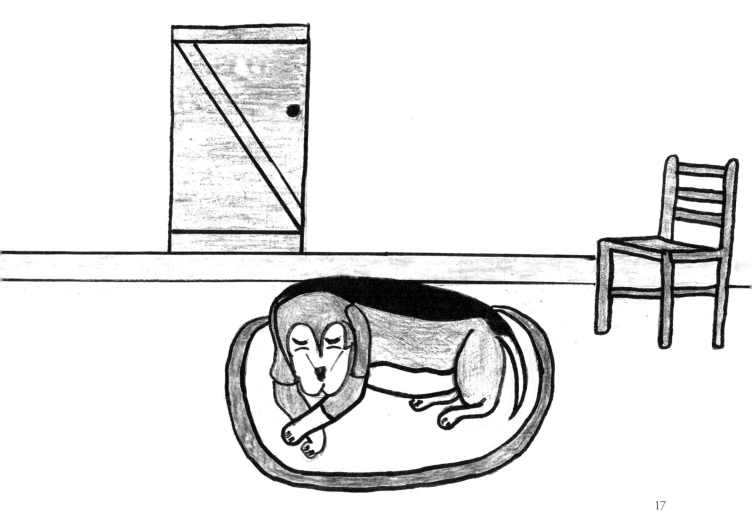

When she arrived home, her human, Taylor greeted her. "Where have you been all day?" she asked. " You must be starving?" " I made you some gravy to pour on your food. I hope you like it!"

She loved it, but she was so full. She did not want to be rude and hurt her feelings, so she ate it.

Lucy's belly was so full! She slowly climbed into her bed and drifted off to sleep dreaming about her adventures for the next day.

The end

Printed in the United States
by Baker & Taylor Publisher Services